Seasonal Sisters

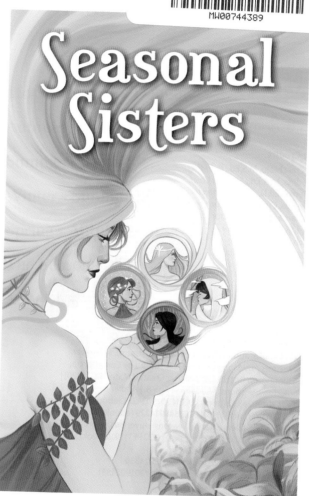

By Monika Davies
Illustrated by Carol Garcia

Mother Nature's Daughters

I am
Mother Nature.
I have daughters,
four of them,
Autumn,
  Summer,
    Winter,
      Spring.

Long, long ago I
nicknamed them my
young seasonal sisters,
who season the
world
in their given time.

But now, now,
I shall ask them to find
themselves in a new season
so they may write anew
and understand new stories.

Autumn's Winter

My Autumn,
she is glowing
merriment
and a warm fire.

And yet,
sometimes I sense
she struggles.

She does not understand
the peace
of a clean slate,
the necessity
of rest.

So I move the Earth,
shift the seasons,
settling my dear daughter
in a
        new
                winter.

❧

I am Autumn, and, when it is my turn
to season the world, I let my imagination
run wild. I walk around with a color
palette in hand. I choose only the warmest
hues—yellow, orange, red. I pick these
colors to remind people of heat before
the winter comes. Some years, I dust
the world in a cacophony of orange and
red leaves. I let the leaves fall, tucked
into piles on the ground. Other years, I
flood the world with yellow-leaved trees,
painting in some last-minute greenery to
slip through the shades.

But, today, on what should be my
opening day of an autumn, I open the door
to find my autumn is—*gone.*

All around me, the world is still and
cold and gray.

And I realize—I am in Winter's land.

Of all my sisters, I understand Winter
the least, for Winter is cold and likes to
glaze the world in a layer of white ice. I

like to douse the world in flames, and she—she ensures the world is kept tidy and tame.

Winter doesn't use a color palette to season the world; instead, she calls upon the clouds. Her clouds find me, circling around and around.

"Will you shower the world in snow?" the clouds ask me. "Are we throwing the world into a deep winter, a deep sleep?"

I am not sure what to do—caught in this season I know nothing of. But then, I think of how Winter has spoken to me in the past. She has whispered to me quietly, so quietly, how she likes the silence of a deep snowfall. How the world is so much gentler when snow has blanketed the world in silence.

"Go gently, gently, then plunge us into a full snowfall," I reply.

The clouds swirl, curling and curling

in and out of the sky, as snow falls, flake after flake, crystal after crystal. I turn my face to the sky. Snowflakes press into my skin. I stick my tongue out, capturing a few flakes.

I breathe deep, and crisp air fills and stretches my lungs.

I let my breath out, a cloud of cold whispering from my lips.

This season is cold, so cold. It is only one color. But I feel a silence in my soul, one that soothes.

As I stand in the snowfall, I wonder if perhaps, perhaps, taking a breath and letting this world stand in silence can help me find peace that's perhaps tougher to find in my autumn.

Remember, my dear Autumn, this is the season of rest, I hear, my Mother Nature's voice a hymn in my ear.

Summer's Spring

My Summer,
she is light
amusement
and a cup overflowing.

And yet,
sometimes I sense
she struggles.

She does not understand
the purpose
of a new beginning,
the wonder
of growth.

So I move the Earth,
shift the seasons,
settling my dear daughter
in a
     new
        spring.

12

I am Summer and I am loud and I am brighter than the twinkle in the eye of the sun.

I love it when it's my chance to season the world. I believe people look best when they wear sunglasses of any size or shape. I am a fan of beaches, turquoise tides, and spiking hot temperatures. I am loud and splashy and very, very happy.

Mother Nature has always said that I'm maybe a little too loud. But here's the thing: I like beaming sunshine everywhere. I like seeing people drenched in sweat, basking in rays of sun. I am loud, and I have a sticker board to perk up the world. My season is happy and I want to sunbathe in those beams of happiness.

But today I wrench open my door to start my season and find instead my summer has—*disappeared*.

All around me the world is calm and bleak and brown.

And I realize—I am in Spring's land.

Now, Spring, that dear, dear sister, is…a dear. Yes, she's gentle and kind. However, she is everything but spice. Her season starts slow and moves slow and ends slow and I have no idea how to move slowly. I like to shine and blind, while Spring is happy to sit and simply shimmer.

And yet—here sits Spring's basket of bulbs on my doorstep.

I am not sure what to do, but I pick up the basket of bulbs. I weigh it in my hands and swing the basket from one arm crook to the other.

I begin to wonder how it will feel to be responsible for new growth and new life. When I season the world, everything I see is fully grown, and I wonder: how will it feel to watch the world turn green and bright and alive?

Then, somehow, I find myself planting Spring's bulbs one by one by one, then two by two by two. I first plant them in rows; then I grow bold and I am flying across the fields, and it almost seems that the ground plucks the bulbs from my fingers.

Then, I wait. I wait so long that my eyelids start to sway, but I keep them open because I want to see this new growth. Then—then—I see tiny sprouts. Their tiny, green heads nudge out of the soil, and they peek and peer upward. I keep my eyes peeled and pressed to their growth, and they lift their limbs and I am entranced.

I wonder what they will look like as they grow tall and taller and tallest.

I wonder if there is a beauty and patience in waiting for growth.

I wonder and I watch and I wait.

Remember, my dear Summer, this is the season of beginnings, I hear, my Mother Nature's voice a hymn in my ear.

Winter's Summer

My Winter,
she is peaceful
softness
and a gentle bluebird.

And yet,
sometimes I sense
she struggles.

She does not understand
the beauty
of feeling seen,
the understanding
of being in the light.

So I move the Earth,
shift the seasons,
settling my dear daughter
in a
      new
         summer.

I am Winter, and I carry secrets. I keep them in my pockets, tucked in envelopes that I seal shut with frost. They are secrets that are mine, and I like to bury them away, far from prying eyes.

Mother Nature says I'm the shiest of my sisters. But it's not that I'm shy. It's only that sometimes I like the private of a quiet, crisp afternoon. Sometimes, I like to sip tea in the hollow of a tree and hide away from the eyes of the world.

I love when it's my turn to season the world. I call upon the clouds to blanket the world in snow. They swing slowly, sure of their purpose, and send flakes from the sky. Once it snows, the world quiets too, and everything turns peaceful.

But today, I pull open my door, ready to begin my season, and find instead my winter has—*vanished.*

All around me, the world is bright and blaring and green.

And I realize—I am in Summer's land.

Summer blazes into every room and shares every thought she thinks. When I have supper with her, she throws open every window and calls every bird and bumblebee to our table. But, for me, I like the peace of a quiet season, when the animals of the world sleep and wait for spring to come.

I am not sure what to do with Summer's sticker board at my feet. There are stickers of palm ferns and surfboards and water slides. The stickers seem to scream brightly to me.

The sun beams brightly everywhere. I feel like there's nowhere to hide. Everything seems louder now—music is blasting over loudspeakers, children are running through sprinklers, and vendors are selling frozen treats.

But I think of Summer, how she loves

her season so dearly. I know I need to see what makes her beam with such cheer. So I decide to walk. I take Summer's sticker board and begin sticking the stickers—a palm tree here, an ice cream stand there.

The sun shines down. I turn my face upward, feeling the warmth washing over me. I ease my hood off my head, and I can feel my hair heat up in the sunshine.

Two kids skate past me, giggling and waving, and I cannot help but wave back. A group of elders is dancing in the nearby square, and my feet tap along. A couple is sipping lemonades across the street, while a young boy asks his dad for an ice cream cone on the other corner.

I take it all in. And I can feel, and almost touch, the joy in the air. The world is so bright and merry in this season, and I can feel my heartbeat quicken, ever so slightly.

Remember, my dear Winter, this is the season to be seen, I hear, my Mother Nature's voice a hymn in my ear.

Spring's Autumn

My Spring,
she is cheerful
grace
and an arching rainbow.

And yet,
sometimes I sense
she struggles.

She does not understand
the possible joy
of a final chapter,
the beauty
behind an ending.

So I move the Earth,
shift the seasons,
settling my dear daughter
in a
      new
         autumn.

I am Spring, and for me, every day is a day to start fresh. I like the whisper and thud of a new beginning, how a new start sometimes springs to life, or begins oh so quietly. I like the smell of fresh dirt, the smell of pavement after rainfall, the smell of grass growing tall. I like to feel new buds under my feet, pink and orange and purple tulips squirming their way to the sky. I like so many things that I hardly know where my list begins or ends.

I always season the world thinking of beginnings. I never like to think of final chapters and endings and the way some things must close.

But today, I slide open my door, so prepared to tackle my season, to find my spring has—*evaporated.*

All around me, the world is dying and glowing and changing color.

And I realize—I am in Autumn's land.

I love my sister Autumn. I love all

my sisters equally, of course. However, Autumn is proud and full of warmth, and views endings as golden sunsets.

I am not sure what to do. I see her color palette, resting on a log. I gingerly pick it up. I examine the colors of red, yellow, and orange—all colors I know, but never spend much time with. It seems like an endless swirl of colors trapped on one wooden board.

I don't want to put the world to sleep. But it seems I must bring in an autumn. So I hold Autumn's palette. I take her paintbrush. I sigh, daunted, but ready to paint the world into yellow and orange and red.

I start slowly, painting a few maple leaves a yellow hue. I then start touching up the leaves on several aspens, blending their greens into yellows. My beautiful aspens light up next to pine trees. I'm

struck by how the world shines in
this season.

I start to paint faster, and faster, and
faster. I'm so eager to see how the world
will change as I keep painting. Paint
flies off my palette, as yellows blend
into oranges, which blend into reds. I
feel like I'm staring at a whole new

world, one alight in a wash of proud and vulnerable colors.

Leaves begin to fall, sprinkling the ground. I feel a little teary at the sight of this ending, as this season of light begins to close its eyes.

But then I think of Autumn and her words to me.

The nature that falls asleep in my season, well, it has lived a full life. It is happy to move on, she said to me once.

Perhaps we can say goodbye while rejoicing in a full life lived.

Remember, my dear Autumn, this is the season for beautiful endings, I hear, my Mother Nature's voice a hymn in my ear.

The Seasonal Sisters

I have daughters,
four of them,
Autumn,
      Summer,
            Winter,
                  Spring.

Each of them crafts
a seasonal story,
and now,
they have written
another story
that was not
once
theirs.

Together,
they will keep
crafting
the stories of the
seasons,
but with new
understanding.
Think of them
when
a leaf falls,
      the sun beams,
           snow drips,
                a flower grows.

They are writing
the fresh seasons
that are
the backdrop
to
your stories
in your world.

About Us

The Author

Monika Davies is a Canadian writer and traveler. She does not have a favorite season as she enjoys them all equally! She loves spring's bright tulips, summer's comfortable heat, autumn's lively color scheme, and winter's tranquility. She graduated with a bachelor of fine arts in creative writing. She has written over 20 books for young readers.

The Illustrator

Carol Garcia is a freelance illustrator from São Paulo, Brazil. She studied advertising, and she then developed her artistic career as an illustrator specializing in digital painting. She often creates inspirational characters with striking colors. She has previously worked to create illustrations for educational children's books in math and English.